The Humming Bird Secret

The Humming Bird Secret

Susan Gates

SCHOLASTIC
PRESS

To Laura

Scholastic Children's Books,
Commonwealth House, 1-19 New Oxford Street,
London WC1A 1NU, UK
a division of Scholastic Ltd
London ~ New York ~ Toronto ~ Sydney ~ Auckland
Mexico City ~ New Delhi ~ Hong Kong

First published in the UK by Scholastic Ltd, 1999

Text copyright © Susan Gates, 1999
Illustrations copyright © Angelo Rinaldi, 1999

ISBN 0 590 11397 6

Typeset by DP Photosetting, Aylesbury, Bucks.
Printed by Cox and Wyman Ltd, Reading, Berks.

10 9 8 7 6 5 4 3 2 1

Contents

Chapter 1
Servants Should Not Steal Treacle

I'm starting to shiver.

"Where are you, Eliza? It's me, Miss Marianne. Answer me! Are you in your bedroom?"

I'm climbing the garret stairs, calling out for Eliza, our servant girl.

"Eliza?"

The stairs are creaky. It's fearfully dark. There's no carpet or gaslight up here. I didn't know that. But I have never been to this part of the house.

Eliza shouldn't be in her bedroom. She

should be in the kitchen, making my dinner. Cook has been called away to her sick mother and Father is visiting the Bishop. But Eliza needn't think she can be idle. I'm Mistress, now the two of us are alone in the house.

But I think I'm a little afraid.

"For shame, Marianne," I scold myself. "There's nothing to fear. Surely you don't fear ghosts or bogeymen? What would Father say?"

Creak. That's not bogeymen or the stairs. That's my boots. They need oiling. Eliza must do it – when I find out where she is.

"Silly goose!" I scold myself again. "You are twelve years old. Nearly grown!"

I haven't been idle, not like Eliza. Father will be very pleased with me. I've been practising my handwriting. (Father says it is very bad.) I've been sewing and learning my Bible verses. Just as if Father were here, watching everything I do.

"Liza?"

I push open her bedroom door. It's empty.

Just a tiny room with grey walls and bare floorboards.

"What a horrible little room!" I exclaim before I can help myself.

I wouldn't like to be up here. Alone at the top of those creaky stairs. What if your candle blew out?

"Marianne!" I warn myself because my heart is beginning to flutter. "Don't give way to childish fears. What would Father say?"

Once, I saw my mother gliding through my bedroom in a white dress. Father said, "Don't be so foolish, child! Your mother is not here. She is with the angels in Heaven."

My hand grips the locket round my neck. It's silver, on a black ribbon. It has a curl of my mother's hair inside. Aunt Hettie gave it to me. But I must wear it in secret, under my dress. For Father wouldn't approve.

"Liza?" I call out in a shaky voice, even though it's plain she isn't here.

What's she got under her bed? I have to crouch down to look. I'm allowed. I am Mistress. And servants shouldn't have secrets from their mistress, should they? But there's only the trunk that came with her from the orphanage. And a cracked chamber pot.

But wait, here's a shiny copper pan.

That doesn't belong here. That belongs in the kitchen. There's sweet, sticky stuff inside. Treacle!

Eliza shouldn't have treacle. Treacle is a special treat, along with jam and sugar. The treats are locked away in a cupboard and Father has the key. Only Father can unlock the sugar cupboard. And Father isn't here.

Suddenly I think of Liza, with her candle blown out, eating treacle to comfort herself. I would need some comforts if I was all alone in the dark. Perhaps servants don't mind. But I would mind. How the wind must moan up here!

But then I remember that I am Mistress. And servants shouldn't steal treacle, should they? I must give her a good telling off. Father would expect it.

There's half a lemon on her washstand. Where did she get that? What business has a servant girl with treacle and lemons? I must scold her about that too.

But where is she?

Suddenly, from far below me, I hear Liza's voice. It sounds awfully urgent.

"Miss Marianne! Miss Marianne, where are you? Come quick!"

Chapter 2
The Package From Jamaica

I go flying down the stairs. Eliza is not hard to find. She's in the hallway, looking at a hamper.

"Miss Marianne," she says, all excited. "Look what's just been delivered."

I try to keep my voice cool. For I am angry, remember, about the treacle and the lemon.

"Who is it for?"

A wild hope is fluttering in my breast. It might be from Aunt Hettie, full of pretty things for me. Perhaps she knows that Father is away. For if Father were here she wouldn't dare send it.

Eliza looks at the label and my hopes are dashed. She says, "It's for your father, Miss. It says, *The Reverend Doctor A.F. Moxton*. The delivery man said it's a very special package. Come all the way from Kingston, Jamaica!"

My father is a Minister of the Church. He also studies Natural History. He often gets packages from foreign lands. Sometimes they have bones inside. Or dead creatures for him to study.

"*Cheep, cheep,*" comes from inside the hamper.

Eliza looks at me with alarm: "Did you hear that, Miss? I heard a noise from inside that basket."

"You are mistaken," I tell her sternly.

But I crouch down to listen.

"*Cheep, cheep, cheep.*"

This is not Father's usual package of bones and dried-up things. There is something alive in there!

"What shall we do, Miss?" asks Eliza.

I am Mistress. So I must decide.

"We must open it," I tell her. But my voice doesn't sound very certain.

"Oh, no!" Eliza is twisting her apron in her hands. She does that when she's upset.

"It's addressed to the Reverend Doctor, Miss. We cannot open it! Not on any account. I'm afraid he'll be awful mad."

Servants shouldn't disagree with their Mistress. I should tell her off. But I can't. Because I'm afraid, too.

There is a silence between us. Both of us are thinking of my father. I see him turn his cold eyes upon us, as he does on the people in church every Sunday.

I hear his stern voice. "Marianne, explain yourself. How dare you meddle with things that don't concern you!"

What to do? Liza and I stare at each other, dismayed. I try to pretend I didn't hear the cheeping. Perhaps I did not. I turn my mind to other things.

"Eliza," I say in my best Mistress voice. "I was up in your bedroom, searching for you. What is that treacle I just happened to see?"

Liza doesn't seem in the least guilty.

"It's the cockroach trap, Miss Marianne. They climb up the pan and tumble into the treacle. Then in the morning, if they ain't dead yet, I fish 'em out and tap 'em with my boot. They make a fearful cracking noise. It makes you squirm to hear it! Cook give me the treacle, Miss. I didn't steal it, honest."

She needn't have told me about that cracking noise. She is far too chatty for a servant.

"I suppose that's all right then, Eliza."

I'm not sure it's all right. Because Father has many rules. But I don't think there's one that says servants must not make cockroach traps.

"*Cheep, cheep,*" comes from inside the hamper.

I pretend not to hear it.

"And what about the lemon?" I ask her.

"Cook was going to throw it out, Miss. So I asked her if I might have it. It's for my hands, Miss. To make them white, like a fine lady's."

I can't help looking at Eliza's hands. They are red and sore from scrubbing floors. It must sting something awful when she rubs lemon juice on them.

"You can have it, if you like," says Eliza. "Lemon juice is good for whitening freckles too."

How dare she mention my freckles! Liza is the same age as me. At least we believe she is, for she comes from an orphanage and doesn't know her birthday. But she is servant and I am Mistress. So my freckles are none of her business!

I should give her a good telling off. But my heart isn't in it. I'm too worried about the package from Jamaica.

"Shall we really open it?" I whisper to Eliza. Eliza's eyes are popping with fear.

"We dare not," she whispers back. "*He* will know, for certain. He knows everything!"

It's true. Father is like God. He knows everything. You can't have any secrets from him.

We sit down on the black and white tiles of the hallway. I'm shivery all over, waiting for the next *cheep, cheep.*

Liza's eyes are fixed on the hamper, too. But she says, "If I was a fine lady, Miss, I would have treats all the time. Like sugarplums. Or drawers made out of pink satin! Not ugly scratchy ones like *these.*

"Whoo!" she goes. And lifts up her dress to show me her drawers!

"Liza!"

I gaze at her, shocked. Pink satin drawers! What business has a servant dreaming of things like that?

But I can't help thinking. I have scratchy grey drawers beneath my dress, too. Liza and I are dressed nearly the same. You can't tell servant from Mistress. We both have ugly, plain clothes.

Father approves of plain clothes.

Aunt Hettie sent me a nightdress, once. Oh, it was so pretty. It had lace ruffles. But Father said I couldn't have it. He burned it in the fire. He made me watch.

"*Cheep, cheep.*"

We both stare boggle-eyed at the hamper.

"Open it, Liza," I order her.

"No, no, Miss. I durstn't. You do it! It is addressed to the Master! I durstn't."

She isn't going to obey me. I should give her a good telling off.

But I just say: "Well, I shall do it then," in my best Mistress voice.

But my hands are shaking very badly. I can hardly pull out the willow stick that fastens the basket.

I lift the lid.

"Oh, Miss!" says Eliza, clasping her hands.

Inside is a mossy nest. And inside that are three little birds. They are like sparkling jewels — all crimson, green and gold. It's a mother bird and her chicks. The chicks are so tiny. Hardly bigger than bees.

"I know what these are," I tell Liza in excitement. "These are the humming birds from Jamaica that Father talked so much about. Do you remember, Liza? He was so anxious for them to arrive."

"They look a bit poorly if you ask me, Miss," says Liza.

I look again. She's right. The mother bird is drooping. The pretty lights on her wings are all going out.

I take her in my hand. She doesn't stir. She's as light as a crispy leaf. . .

I don't know what to do. I'm afraid to crush her. I put her back in the nest.

"Liza," I say in a helpless whisper. "I do believe Father's humming birds are dying."

"Do something quick," begs Liza. "Master will be fearful mad if they do die! He will punish us, for certain!"

Chapter 3
A Rainbow Dazzle

My heart is sinking like a stone.

I can hear Father's voice in my head: "Marianne, this is most displeasing! How came my birds to die? You have neglected your duty most shamefully!"

Father loves the wonders of Nature. He studies them. If we let his birds die he will not forgive us. He will punish us.

I know what he will do to me. His hot anger will not last long. But his cold anger will. It will last for weeks, or even months. He will never forgive, no matter how much I beg. He will not speak one single word to me. He will not even look at me. He will look straight through me. As if I was a ghost-child.

Liza's little pale face is even paler. She wants me to save her from Father's anger. But I don't know anything about humming birds. I am Mistress but I don't know what to do.

"Where does the Master keep his study key?" I ask Eliza. "He has many books in his study. One may tell me how to save the humming birds."

"You can't go into Master's study, Miss," says Liza, very shocked. "What if he should find out? You know it ain't allowed."

"Father isn't due back for two days yet."

But Liza is right. I'm not allowed into Father's study. That is one of his strictest rules.

He keeps the door locked.

Once, by mistake, he left it open. I peeked in, with my heart beating fast. I saw lots of books. And a wooden bench with strange glass tubes and flasks. Then I heard his footstep. And I ran away in case he caught me.

"Oh, Miss!" wails Liza. "I'm so afraid."

I am, too.

"Shhh, shhh!" I tell her, pointing at the humming birds.

But the little pets don't seem to mind us. They're a pitiful sight — just tiny scraps of feathers. They're not chirping any more. The mother bird has closed her eyes.

"Wait, wait," I tell Eliza. "I've remembered something Father said. He said humming birds drink nectar from flowers."

"So must we take them into the garden, Miss?"

"No, no, they might fly away. Then what will Father say? We'll take them to the conservatory."

I dash through the drawing room to the conservatory. Eliza comes behind with the hamper.

"Make haste!" I cry, wild with impatience. "Come on, Liza! Don't be a slowcoach."

Then I remember what a precious burden she carries.

"No, no," I call back. "Take all the time in the world. Just don't drop them!"

I push open the conservatory door. It smells hot and flowery inside.

Our conservatory is like a big glass tent. It's very high, high as a circus tent nearly. And it's a jungle of plants. There are pineapples and bananas and passion fruit in here. Do such things grow in Jamaica?

I don't know. Father won't allow me to go to school. He teaches me lessons. But there are many things he says I do not need to know.

"Liza! What a time you're taking!"

The humming birds will feel at home in here. They will get better. They must get better. They must.

Liza arrives at last. She sets the hamper down

on a stone bench. The one with the lion's feet.

"Fly!" I command the humming birds. "Fly and feed on the flowers!"

They're not taking the slightest notice of my orders.

"They're not flying, Miss," says Liza.

"I can see that. I think they're too weak."

Poor little weary travellers, they have come such a long way. They don't have the strength even to lift their heads.

There's a plant just above my head. I tear some of the white flowers from it. Then poke them into the nest with my finger.

"Please take some food," I beg them. "Please don't die. You mustn't die. Father will be very angry with you."

Suddenly, a rainbow dazzle shoots past my eyes.

"Look, Liza!"

It's the mother humming bird. She hangs sparkling in the air. Just like a jewel!

Then, flash, she is somewhere else. Where though?

"There, Miss, there!" cries Eliza. "It makes me giddy to watch her! Oh, how pretty!"

And then Liza makes a terrible mistake. She is so delighted she claps her hands. She can't help it.

The mother bird is startled. She darts again. She dashes herself against the glass. Then tumbles to the ground.

"Oh, no! Close the lid, Liza. Close the lid quick so the babies don't fly!"

Liza drops to her knees. She is sobbing as if her heart will break. Her face is all wet with tears.

"Oh Miss, oh Miss, is it dead? I can't look. Is it dead?"

I kneel down by the mother humming bird. All her beautiful lights have gone out. I pick her up with great care, praying she might be alive.

"Please, please, let her still be alive."

But she lies quite still in my palm.

She is dead.

"She's cold!" cries Eliza, frantic. "She is just cold, Miss. That's all."

She grabs the tiny body. She stuffs it under the bib of her apron, against her skinny chest, to try to warm it into life.

"Liza," I say very gently. "It's quite, quite dead. Its neck is broken. Give it back to me."

"It might come alive, Miss!"

"It's no use. Please give it back."

She gives me the bundle of feathers. It's light as a puff of wind. I lay it down on the stone bench. And both of us stand gazing at it, with horror in our hearts.

"Oh, Miss," cries Eliza. "Look what I've done. Look what I've done to Master's humming bird! I will lose my place, Miss. The Master will send me away. Where will I go, Miss? I've got nowhere else to go."

And she starts rocking to and fro, to and fro, as if she's in terrible pain.

Her thin shoulders are shaking. I put my arms

round them and give her a big hug. Father wouldn't approve. When he is here Liza stays in the kitchen. She uses the back stairs. We hardly ever see each other.

"Oh, Miss Marianne," she sobs. "What are we to do?"

I have made a decision. But it's hard to stop my voice from trembling.

"Don't fret, Liza," I tell her. "I shall tell the Master. You shan't get into trouble. I'll take all the blame."

Then my heart gives a great leap. I pull my arms from Liza's shoulders and rush to the conservatory window. I thought I heard Father's carriage wheels on the drive! Father drives a high, black carriage with high spinning wheels. It has a hood that closes over it. The hood is as black and shiny as a cockroach.

But the carriage isn't there. I was hearing things. Father's visiting the Bishop. He isn't due back for two days yet.

"We had better hide the mother bird," I tell Eliza.

I dig her a grave in a big plant pot. We lay her in and pat the soil over her.

I daren't mark the place with a cross in case Father sees it. So I lay a white flower on the top.

Poor little motherless birds, I think, looking at the hamper.

I feel dreadfully sad. But I don't say anything, for that would set Liza off again. And she is sorry enough already.

I don't think the babies will live long. But I daren't tell Eliza that. Instead I say, "Perhaps we can save the other two, then Father will not mind so much. So long as he has two of them to study."

Father has been waiting for them a long, long time. He will be so pleased with me. If only I can keep them alive until he comes home.

Chapter 4
Into the Lion's Den

I'm in the drawing room, trying to think what to do. Liza is in the kitchen, making us some bread and milk. Bread and milk is for supper really and it isn't suppertime yet. But since the humming birds came everything has gone topsy-turvy. Nothing is orderly, as Father likes it to be.

"I should be scrubbing the steps now," Liza says to me.

"And I should be learning the Kings and Queens of England," I tell her.

But how can I learn about Kings and Queens, when the humming bird chicks are dying?

I keep looking at the hamper, on the stone bench in the conservatory. I daren't lift the lid, in case they are dead already.

"Miss," says Eliza, coming in with the bread and milk. "Do you want plum jam with this? I know where the Master hides the key to the cupboard."

Liza isn't at all shy. She seems to have come alive since Father left, like a little bubbling spring. She chats away all the time. Almost as if we were friends.

Father would have a fit. He said that my mother was too friendly with servants. That she spent too much time in the kitchen, chatting with Cook. He said he even heard them *laughing* together.

I answer sternly, "No, Eliza. Father would not like us having jam without his permission."

And she says, "Don't get all highty-tighty

again, Miss. Just when we was getting on so splendid."

I have to blush. I didn't know I was highty-tighty.

Liza says, "Lemons is good for blushing, Miss. Did you know that? Good for blushing and freckles."

"Hush," I tell her. "You do prattle, Liza." But I'm smiling when I say it.

I should smile more, Aunt Hettie says. She says I'm too grave and sad. She says I should be light-hearted and merry like my mother was. Until she married my father. She married when she was only sixteen. And Father was already old.

"Shall I go back in the kitchen, Miss?" Liza asks me.

"No, no, stay here, Liza."

We sit down and eat our bread and milk together. We stick our feet up on the fender to warm our boots at the fire.

Liza says, "Do you get chilblains, Miss? I suffer with 'em something cruel."

I'm eating with servants now. We're warming our boots and talking about our chilblains!

Father would be hopping mad. "I see your mother's faults in you! I thought I had trained you better!" he would roar at me.

But it's so lonely not having someone to talk to and this is such a big, gloomy house. And I'm sick with worry over those humming birds. I'm sure they won't live. Not now their poor mother is dead.

Liza says, as if she can read my mind, "Those humming birds is a terrible worry, ain't they, Miss?"

"You should not have clapped and killed their mother!"

"Oh, Miss, I didn't mean to. Honest I didn't! I couldn't help myself. It's just that humming bird when it flew, Miss, I've never seen nothing so lovely."

I've made her cry now. I wish I hadn't said it.

"Oh, Miss," she sobs. "What are we doing to do?"

I've made a decision. But just thinking about it chills my heart.

"I've got to go into Father's study, Liza. There are books there. There may be one about humming birds. We may find out how to save them."

Liza sniffs and wipes a drip off her nose. "I know where he keeps the key." She points to the mantelpiece. "It is behind the clock, with the sugar cupboard key."

I stare at the clock. *Tick tock, tick tock.* A lot of tick tocks pass before I get out of my chair and say: "I am going then."

"It's the big iron key," says Liza. "Not the tiny one."

My boots are heavy as lead. The key feels like a piece of ice in my hand. With my other hand I'm gripping my mother's locket very tight.

"I am going then."

It feels like I'm going into the lion's den.

I do it all in a rush. I run upstairs and twist the key in the lock and scurry inside. I don't dare raise my head. It would be wrong to look about. This is Father's private place where he mustn't be disturbed. He even eats his meals in here.

What's that strange smell? What is it? Such a nasty stink. It makes my nose twitch.

Here's his desk. Keeping my eyes low I peek at what's on it. There's a leather wallet. It's open. There are tiny clamps and tweezers. Rows of miniature scalpels, all sharp and shining. How curious. What surgeon would use these? They would only do to cut open a very tiny patient. . .

No time to wonder. Father would not like me spying. My eyes dart over his books. And straight away I see it. A red book called *Humming Birds*. I grab it from the shelves and open it.

Then all at once I start shaking violently. I

nearly drop the book. I know Father's away. But it feels like he's here. Watching me do forbidden things. Watching me read his books! I dare not look up. But I can see his stone-cold stare. I can hear his voice.

"Wretched girl! Explain yourself. What are you doing here?"

I run outside and lock the room up again.

Then I collapse on the stairs. I take some deep breaths to clear my lungs of that foul stink.

"He isn't here," I keep telling myself in a slow, calm voice. "He is visiting the Bishop. He will not be home for two days yet."

But it takes a long while to stop shaking.

Then I open Father's book again. And straight away I'm enchanted.

It's the most beautiful book I've ever seen. There are pictures of humming birds. The pictures sparkle, like sequins. The humming birds glow as if they were alive.

I turn the pages. Their names sound like poetry. Azure crowned, amethyst, ruby throated...

I stop at that picture.

"Those are ours," I murmur to myself. "Ours are crimson and green and gold like that."

Our humming birds are ruby throated. I must tell Liza. Here's some writing about them. I begin to read. Soon I'm reading faster, faster, racing through the pages.

Then I leap up from the stairs in great excitement.

"Liza! Liza! I know how to save the humming birds!"

Chapter 5
This Ain't America, Is It?

"Listen to this!" I shout to Liza as I go rushing down the stairs. "This book tells about a gentleman in America. It says how he kept humming birds alive in his conservatory. How he made them tame. It says here how he did it!"

Liza looks amazed, as if she can't believe I've come out safe from the lion's den.

"You're back, Miss," she says, in a wondering voice.

"Do pay attention, Liza! We can do what he did. See here, it gives his home-made recipe for nectar. Two parts of loaf sugar, one part treacle, ten parts water."

"I can make that, Miss," says Liza. "Easy peasy."

"Get the key to the cupboard. Hurry, Liza!"

We are breaking Father's rules. Only he is allowed to unlock the sugar cupboard.

But, this time, I don't give a thought to what Father will say. Liza doesn't, either.

"Right, Miss," she says, dashing off.

Liza snatches the key from behind the clock and races to the kitchen.

I follow her with the humming-bird book: "Wait for me!"

It's gloomy down in the kitchen. There are copper pans gleaming on the walls and big stone sinks and wooden tables. I look about, helpless. I don't know where anything is. But Liza does. She darts about getting things from here, from there. She disappears into the sugar cupboard and comes out with a big block of sugar that glitters like snow.

"How much sugar did it say, Miss? Get me a cup."

Liza shouldn't be giving *me* orders. But there's no time to scold her. I open the nearest cupboard door and find a white cup with a silver rim.

"Here's one."

"That there is Cook's best china, Miss," Eliza says sternly. "She'll be awful mad."

Then her lips twitch and she gives a big smile: "But Cook ain't here, is she?"

We stir the home-made nectar with a silver teaspoon.

Liza looks into the cup: "Is this going to work, do you reckon, Miss?"

"It worked for the gentleman in America."

"But this ain't America, is it, Miss? This is England."

We take the humming-bird book and Cook's best china cup back to the conservatory.

"Open the hamper, Liza." I am giving the orders now.

"No, I durstn't, Miss. I couldn't bear it. What if they're dead!"

"Well, I'm not going to open it. You must do it!"

She gives a quick, stubborn shake of her head.

She isn't going to do what she's told.

For a long time, nothing happens. We just stand and stare at each other. Her face is white and full of horror. I expect mine is, too. Neither of us wants to lift the lid for fear of what we might find.

To put off the evil moment, I consult the book again.

Then I drink from the cup and smear some sugary stuff on my lips.

Liza just gawps at me. She probably thinks I've lost my mind.

"That's not for you, Miss. That's nectar for them birds. What are you doing drinking it?"

"It says here you can feed humming birds from your own mouth. It says they dip in their beaks. And feed just like they do from a flower."

"Urgh! I shouldn't care what it says, Miss. It ain't hygienic."

"But we must try everything we can to save them."

Liza frowns horribly and twists her apron.

At last she decides: "I'll open the hamper then."

I'm really grateful to her. She's braver than me. I couldn't open that hamper. Not for a thousand pounds.

"But I ain't going to look inside, Miss. I'm going to keep my eyes closed."

Liza creeps towards the hamper. She reaches out her hand and screws her eyes tight shut. . .

"Wait, Liza, wait! It says something else. It says, 'Don't be deceived by humming birds.

They are not as timid as they seem.' It says they're very bold. That they fight like furies. They attack eagles, even people."

Liza's eyes shoot open. "I don't believe it, Miss."

"They dart at people's faces and stab them. Sometimes blind them with their long bills. It says their bills are sharp as needles."

But Liza isn't listening. She's closed her eyes again and is feeling about for the hamper lid. She finds it and opens it.

"Are the humming birds alive?"

"I told you, Miss, I ain't looking."

Her eyes are still shut tight.

I take another sip from the china cup. And wait.

Nothing happens. Nothing flies out of the hamper.

They have died then.

Suddenly, all the world seems black and hopeless.

Then, whizz, there is a whirring sound. My head turns this way, that way. What is it?

It's them! They are here. I didn't see them fly.

They hang in the air like fiery sparks, right in front of my face. They might stab me! I almost flinch, almost beat them away. But I make myself stay still. Very, very still. I can see their needle bills. They look awful pointy.

Their wings are just a golden blur. Their bright black eyes are looking deep into mine.

Then they dart forwards! I close my eyes. But they don't attack. When I open my eyes they are so close all I can see is a gold and crimson glitter.

"Oh Miss, Miss, just look!" whispers Eliza. "Ain't that a sight?"

This time she doesn't shout or clap her hands. She knows that would bring disaster.

"They're drinking food from your mouth," says Eliza in a voice full of wonder.

They're so delicate I can't even feel them. I

daren't speak or even take a breath for fear I might puff them away.

The humming birds whizz off, like tiny shooting stars. They sit and preen their feathers in the banana tree.

"Oh, how pretty," says Liza very, very softly.

It's like a miracle. I'm so happy I can scarcely speak.

"They didn't hurt you, did they, Miss?" says Liza.

"No. They're gentle creatures."

"That there book don't know what it's talking about, does it, Miss?"

"They wouldn't hurt me," I tell Liza. "They are my friends, my little pets."

Then I remember they're not mine at all. They belong to Father. And when he comes home in two days' time he'll want them back.

Chapter 6
A Cure For Sadness

I am in my bedroom, brushing my hair one hundred times. I suffer torments with my hair. It gets into knots and tangles. It won't be tidy. It sticks out like a broom.

I wish I had hair like Liza. She's as skinny as a stick with a little moon face. But she has hair like a fairytale princess. It's brown and silky. It never gets into knots.

Liza is going to sleep here with me. It's not that I'm afraid. I'm too grown-up for that. But I don't want her to be alone in that horrible cold little room, right at the top of the house, where the wind moans.

My humming birds are safe in the conservatory. I'm thinking about them while I brush my hair.

After they had drunk nectar from my lips they got tamer and tamer. Just like Father's book said. They weren't afraid of us at all. I held up the china cup. And they darted round it like sparkling butterflies. They dipped their long bills into it and drank.

"Ninety-nine, one hundred."

I've just reached one hundred brush strokes and I'm about to kneel down and say my prayers when Liza comes into the bedroom.

"I've locked up the house, Miss," she says. "We are all safe and secure."

"We should be in bed by now," I remind her. "Nine o'clock is my bedtime. That's Father's rule."

She is carrying something in a jug.

"I've made some gingerade, Miss," she says.

"I had to use some sugar. But I've put the key back behind the clock."

I shouldn't mind. We have already raided the sugar cupboard for the humming birds. But I keep hearing it – the crunch of carriage wheels on the drive. And I keep seeing Father, whisking in in his black cloak. "Wretched girl! Account for yourself! What has been going on here while I have been away?"

I take a last peep in the mirror. I almost expect to see Father looking over my shoulder. But there is no one there. I try to think of something else.

"What is the best cure for spots, Liza?"

Sometimes I despair of my looks. I have frizzy, brown hair and freckles. And spots under my fringe.

Liza says, "Well, I know a cure. Though I don't absolutely believe it. They say, if your mother passes her gold wedding ring over the spots, they will go away."

Without thinking, I grasp my mother's locket tight.

"Oh, I'm so sorry, Miss," says Liza, her hand flying to her mouth. "I forgot you ain't got a mother."

"Neither have you," I tell her.

We sit in bed under the quilt drinking gingerade.

I ask Liza, "Do you know anything at all about your mother?"

"No," says Liza. "I was left on the doorstep of the orphanage when I was a baby. There was no note or nothing. So they called me Eliza. It's a horrible name, ain't it, Miss? I should have liked to have been called Clarissa, or Marianne like you."

"My father doesn't like my name," I tell her. "He wanted to call me Hepzibah, you know, out of the Bible. But my mother was so ill that he had to give in to her."

"Can't you remember anything about your

mother?" Liza asks me. "Not the least thing?"

We are speaking freely now, like best friends. No one would know who was Mistress and who was servant. Father would be shocked.

"Father hardly speaks of her. All I know is from Aunt Hettie. She is my mother's sister. She's kind, I like her. But I don't see her often. Father doesn't approve. He says she is too like my mother. That she would be a bad influence. She gave me this locket with my mother's hair inside it."

"That's very pretty hair, Miss Marianne," says Eliza.

"Aunt Hettie says my mother was very pretty. And very kind. She had a smile for everyone. She was only seventeen, you know, when she died... And, by the way, Liza, you need not call me Miss when we are alone. But when Father comes home, if he is listening..."

I don't have to say any more. Liza understands. Everything must be as it was before, when Father comes home. All his rules must be obeyed.

"We had better go to sleep now," I tell her. "It's late. Well past nine o'clock."

Liza blows out the candle. We snuggle down in the bed.

"I do remember something. . ." I tell Liza.

"About what, Miss?" she asks me sleepily.

"About my mother. At least I think I do. I remember her lifting me on her knee. I remember cuddling up close under her shawl. I remember she smelled of violets. But I don't suppose I remember it really. For she died soon after I was born."

I give a deep sigh, I can't help it.

"Liza? You know lots of cures, for freckles and spots and things. Do you know a cure for sadness?"

"Gingerade, Miss," says Liza in a dreamy voice.

"Liza?"

No answer.

All I can hear is Liza's gentle breathing. I pull the quilt up over her shoulders. Her princess's hair is spread out all over the pillow. She is worn out, poor soul. She is already fast asleep.

Chapter 7
A Cockroach-Black Carriage

"Father is coming home tomorrow!" That's the first thing that pops into my head when I wake up.

This is the last day I'll be free to talk and laugh with Liza. Father will soon put a stop to that.

I can't bear to think about it. It's breaking my heart.

So I think instead of how Father will be when he sees the humming birds. He'll be so pleased. He may even be kind to me.

He'll watch them, just as we do. Watch all their pretty little ways. How they feed from the china cup and from my lips. He'll soon love them as much as we do.

"Marianne, you mustn't laze about in bed," I tell myself sternly.

I promised Father to rise early, to have a cold sponge bath and learn my Kings and Queens.

Bang, bang, bang!

Someone is pounding on the big front door.

"Father," I whisper in terror.

I am not even dressed yet! Liza is still asleep under the quilt! She should have been up before dawn, lighting the stove, setting the fires. I didn't have the heart to wake her. What will Father say if he sees the fires are cold?

I shake Liza's thin shoulders. "Liza! Liza!"

She groans and rubs her knuckles in her eyes.

"Wake up! Make haste! The Master is back early!"

I leap out of bed and throw a shawl round my shoulders. Then fly over the cold floor in my bare feet, push the window up and stick my head out.

It's Martha from the farm, bringing the milk. She usually leaves it with Cook in the kitchen. But Cook isn't back yet.

I'm so pleased it's Martha and not Father that I can't help laughing out loud.

"Miss, Miss, who is it?"

Liza comes rushing to my side, her hair all over her face and her little bony feet sticking out under her nightdress.

"It's not the Master, is it? It's not the Reverend Doctor? It's already daylight and my work ain't even started yet! I ain't even lit the kitchen stove!"

Her eyes are staring wide in panic. Her face is white as a flour bin. "Oh Miss, why didn't you wake me?"

"It's all right, Liza. I made a mistake. It's not Father back early. It's only Martha with the milk."

She puffs out a big sigh. "Phew. Thank the Lord, Miss," she says.

She's forgotten I told her to call me Marianne. I don't remind her. Thinking of Father's return has cast dark shadows over us both.

Then, suddenly, I think of my humming birds. They'll be awake now. Whizzing about the conservatory like shooting stars.

"Let's go and see the humming birds."

Liza and I pull on our clothes. I puff some breath on my mother's locket and polish it so it shines. I must remember to hide it, when Father comes home. I don't know if he would take it from me. But it's all I have left of my mother so I dare not take the chance.

We go rushing to the conservatory and search about among the green leaves and flowers.

"Where are they, Miss?" asks Liza, alarmed.

Then we hear a soft chirping sound, like grasshoppers.

"There they are, in the banana tree!"

There's a red and gold *fizz* like a firework.

One is sitting on my finger! Just sitting there as if it's his favourite perch.

We watch each other curiously. He isn't frightened of me at all.

"He knows you, Miss," says Liza.

He starts preening his emerald wings, calm as calm.

The other comes flitting round our heads. They seem to trust us. They know we won't let any harm come to them.

They look so pretty. I can't believe they would attack people. Even blind them with their bills.

"Look, Liza," I say, delighted. "Look how tame they're becoming."

"It said so in the book, didn't it, Miss? It said they would."

Father's book. I feel suddenly anxious. "Where is that book, Liza?"

It's there, lying on the stone bench. I pick it up.

"Liza, I must put this back in the study before tomorrow when Father comes home."

My father has a very sharp eye. He would know straight away if it was missing.

"It says in this book, Liza, that the gentleman in America made a little straw cage for his humming birds."

"A cage, Miss? He didn't shut them up, did he?"

"Only at night time. In the day he left the door open and they flew in and out as they pleased. But when it got dark he closed their door. And they felt safe inside. They felt that nothing could hurt them.

"Then we must make one for our birds, too."

We spend all morning making a little cage out of straw. Liza trims it with flowers. Then she stands on a bucket on top of the stone bench.

And hangs the new house as high as she can reach in the banana tree.

"See, they like it!" says Liza, as one flies straight in to inspect it.

The door is wide open. They zip in and out to feed on the nectar in the china cup.

Liza and I sit side by side to watch them. Hours pass. But we don't even notice.

It's as if we are in our secret forest, full of flowers and magical creatures. They flash about us. Then hang in the air like glittering rainbows. Our eyes are dazzled. Every second their colour changes with the light.

"I think they must come straight from Heaven, Miss," whispers Liza. Her little moon face is lit up with smiles.

I can't see my face. But I know it's smiling, too. I wish Aunt Hettie could see me.

Suddenly, Liza pinches my hand very hard.

"Ow, Liza, that hurts!"

She pinches even harder. "What's that

noise?" she says, staring about like a frightened rabbit.

Then I hear it, too. A crunching sound on the gravel drive.

My heart almost stops. It can't be him. He shouldn't be back until. . .

Crunch.

I leap up and rush into the drawing room. I can see a carriage through the tall windows. It's a cockroach-black carriage.

"Liza, it's Father. He's back a day early!"

"Oh no, Miss!"

"Shhh, Liza."

Liza stuffs her fist against her mouth to stop herself crying out.

The hood is up. It's folded over the carriage, like shiny beetles' wings. But I can see inside. The carriage is empty.

Father is already somewhere in the house.

Chapter 8
Keep a Cool Head, Marianne

The spell of our secret forest is broken.

"Quick, quick!" I shoo Liza away like a chicken.

She goes scurrying back to the kitchen.

I daren't even call out goodbye.

For Father's here. He's searching for me: "Marianne! Where are you?"

I can hear footsteps. His voice is getting nearer.

"Marianne, what is the meaning of this? Why is no one here to welcome me?"

Just in time, I stuff Mother's locket back inside my dress. I almost forgot!

Father comes striding into the room in a black travelling cloak. His black top hat and gloves are in his hand.

He throws his gloves towards a chair. He holds out his top hat. No servant is there to take it.

"Where is that girl?" he says, looking about.

His lips are pressed tight together. That means he is not pleased.

Suddenly, I spy something dreadful. Father's humming-bird book is on the table. It's there, plain as day, for Father to see. How could I be so careless? I never put it back in his study!

I rush to take Father's hat and place it on the table, right on top of the humming-bird book.

"Liza's in the kitchen, Father, attending to her duties."

Father nods. "Ahhh, I see," he says, very, very slowly.

But, all the time, his sharp eyes are peering about. His sharp nose is quivering. As if it's sniffing out all of the rules we've broken.

I'm frantic with worry. That gingerade jug is still in my bedroom. I haven't learned my Kings and Queens. But, worst nightmare of all, that book is here. Right under his nose.

If he finds it, he'll know I unlocked his study.

Two little voices are whispering in my ear. One says: "Quick, quick, run away!" But the other says: "Keep a cool head, Marianne."

"Welcome home, Father. There's a package come for you."

I'm trying very hard to keep a cool head. But I can't stop my voice trembling.

His eyes turn slowly round and stare at me. Father has pale green eyes, like gooseberries.

"What did you say, child?"

"There are some humming birds come for you, Father. All the way from Kingston, Jamaica."

"My specimens!" says Father. "At last. I had almost given them up. Where have you put them? Quickly, quickly, child, show me where they are."

Chapter 9
Leave Them In My Hands

It's wonderful. We are sitting side by side on the stone bench, watching the humming birds' dazzling flight.

I've shown Father how they drink from my lips. How they come and perch on my finger. And Father is in a good mood! My little pets have charmed him, too.

It's sad that Liza isn't here. That she must stay in the kitchen. But Father is so pleased that he doesn't mind about Cook being gone since yesterday. He hasn't even asked how I passed the time.

But he does wonder about something. "Were they not sending me three specimens?" he asks himself, looking about.

My heart gives a great leap. I can't help looking at the big flower pot where the mother bird is buried.

But Father doesn't suspect anything.

He says, "It doesn't matter. Two will suit my purposes."

And his lips bend upwards. Father is smiling!

The fear I felt about him coming back is leaking away drop by drop. Is it possible? Have the humming birds worked their magic on him? Has he become kinder and more loving?

It must be true because he says, "Marianne, you have done well."

He almost pats my head. Except he pulls his hand back at the last moment. But I feel as light as a bubble. As if all my cares have melted away.

Perhaps, in his kindly mood, Father will give way a little. Perhaps he will let me chat to Liza sometimes?

But I know that is asking far too much. That is asking for the moon and stars.

He watches the humming birds flash in and out of their little house. Then he stretches his long legs.

(My Father has long, thin legs like stove pipes. His bony fingers are very long, too. Sometimes, he makes the knuckles crack.)

He says, "That is an interesting contrivance." He's pointing at the straw cage.

"Who gave you the idea for that?" he asks me. And his knuckles go crack, crack.

Instantly, I remember the red book in the drawing room under his hat. How could I have forgotten it? How could I sit here being so dreamy when that book *must* be put back?

Father is tired of watching. He seems impatient. He's getting up! He stands right beneath the straw house and shakes the banana tree.

"Take care, Father," I tell him. "You'll startle them. They do not like strangers. They must get used to you first."

His face grows dark and stern and I think, I've made him angry!

But then he smiles.

"They will soon get used to me," he says. He sits down on the stone bench again.

I hardly dare ask him a question. Father is not a man you question. But I want to keep him here so he doesn't go into the drawing room and pick up his hat.

"Father," I ask him, "what is it you wish to study about the humming birds?"

He approves of my question! His gooseberry eyes light up with eagerness.

"Ahhhh," he says. "I wish to settle an old argument. Many scholars say that such birds exist only on nectar from flowers. But I say that is *not* true. I believe they also eat insects – spiders and beetles. I intend to write a paper. I have the title in mind already, *The Nutrition of Humming Birds. The Truth Revealed.* By the Reverend Doctor Arthur Francis Moxton."

My father sounds very proud when he says the title of his paper.

"And will the paper be important, Father? Will many people read it?"

"Oh yes, child," says Father.

He seems delighted that I have asked. He cracks his knuckles and smiles at me.

"It will be published in important journals. I believe it will make me quite famous."

I feel such a glow inside when Father smiles at me.

Then he coughs and says, "Where's that servant girl? My throat is full of dust. I need tea after my long journey."

"I'll tell her, Father."

Here is my chance to put back the book.

But I can't help lingering. Somehow I don't want to leave the humming birds with anyone else. Even Father.

Father sees it and waves me away.

"You may go, Marianne," he says. "You have done well. You may go back to your other duties. Leave them in my hands."

Father stretches his long, bony fingers.

"Yes, Father."

I run off and grab the book on my way, hiding it under my pinafore.

I lift Father's study key from behind the clock. Before it felt like ice. Now it feels like fire in my hand. I am frantic to put that book back.

But I must order his tea first. So I go running down to the kitchen.

Liza is at the sink. She is scrubbing away at some pots and pans.

"I can't get this grease off, Miss," she says, close to tears.

"Never mind that. My father wants tea."

My voice is too stern and unfriendly. I don't mean it to be. But I don't want waiting for his tea to spoil Father's good mood.

Liza turns round and wipes her hands on her apron. Her hands are sore and bleeding. She gives me a timid little smile.

But I must not chat. What if Father hears us? He has ears as sharp as a bat's. His boots are the softest leather – you can't hear him creeping about.

I look over my shoulder and whisper quickly, "Liza, he is in a good mood!"

Liza nods, "Phew, that's a relief."

She pushes her princess's hair out of her eyes. Then rushes over to the big black oven range to put the kettle on the fire.

"It will be ready in two ticks, Miss Marianne," she says, in a meek voice in case Father is listening.

We stare helplessly at each other. But already there's a distance grown between us.

"I'll talk to you soon. I'll find a way. I promise," I whisper.

Liza nods. But she won't look at me. I know she doesn't believe me. Even I don't believe I can keep my promise.

I leave her clinking the tea things and rush off again. The book feels like a heavy weight. The key is scorching my hand.

As I pass the drawing-room door I call to Father: "Your tea is coming, Father!"

To say the truth, I'm thinking more of him than I am of Liza. I want to do and say more things that please him. I want him to praise me again.

Perhaps, I'm thinking, as I tiptoe upstairs to his study, Father is really changed.

Perhaps the humming birds have the power to give people loving hearts.

Chapter 10
The Humming Birds Are In Danger!

I unlock Father's study door and push it open. That smell again – it clutches at my throat.

I scurry to his bookcase and push the humming-bird book into place. I didn't mean to look up. I didn't mean to spy. But by mistake, my eyes slip sideways.

And what I see makes my blood turn cold as ice.

There's a wooden bench, criss-crossed with cuts. And on it are flasks and tubes and glass jars.

It is what's in the jars that makes me gasp out loud with horror.

There's a rat with eyes like milky marbles. He's pickled in yellow liquid. You can see his insides. They're pinned down with little red pins.

Next to him, there's a long white worm curled into a glass tube. And in the next jar floats a tiny shrivelled heart.

These must be the creatures Father has studied.

Here's a stuffed robin in a case. His breast is still red as a poppy. His beak is open as if he's still singing. I go closer.

There's some tiny cramped handwriting on his case.

"Robin, *Erithacus rubecula*, trapped in woodland by A.F. Moxton, May 6th, 1886."

Father trapped this robin last week.

But I still can't believe it.

I whirl around. Father's tiny scalpels and knives are ready on his desk.

"No," I tell myself, shaking my head. "He wouldn't harm my pets."

Then I catch sight of the humming bird. He's in a glass case on a high shelf. Trembling, I go closer and stand on tiptoe to look.

The poor thing is stuck on a twig with blobs of yellow glue. His emerald feathers are dusty. There's no sparkle left. His bill has snapped off and fallen to the floor of the case...

Bang! That's the front door slamming.

I'm startled awake, as if from a terrible dream.

I go flying down the stairs: "Father!"

Liza is in the drawing room, holding the tea tray and looking bewildered.

"The Master has just gone out, Miss. Doesn't he want his tea?"

I can't see Father out of the tall windows. I climb on to a chair so I can see over our garden wall. There he is, striding across the village green. He's going to the chemist's shop. Father buys lots of chemicals. He says he needs them for his studies.

"Liza, I can't see properly. Has he got the humming birds with him? Was he carrying anything?"

"I don't think so, Miss. What's wrong? You look as white as chalk."

"Liza, our humming birds aren't safe with Father. He means to harm them. I'm almost certain."

"No, Miss!"

With a great clatter, Liza drops the tea tray. Tea spoons and sugar lumps go hopping over the carpet.

"Oh, look what I've done now! That teacup is cracked. That's Cook's best china, that is."

She kneels down and begins to crawl about, picking up the tea things.

"Never mind that, Liza. The humming birds are in danger!"

Both of us dash to the conservatory.

"Where are they?"

I look wildly round. I can't see them. Surely Father hasn't taken them away?

"There they are, Miss. Up there," whispers Liza.

They are high up in the glass roof. Their wings are whirring, like tiny clockwork jewels. The light makes them glitter crimson, emerald, gold.

"They're so gorgeous, Miss," says Liza. "Surely the Master couldn't hurt them?"

Then we gaze at each other in silent horror. For we both know he could.

"But how does he mean to hurt them, Miss?"

Before I can answer, the humming birds come darting down to see us. They aren't a bit afraid. They hover inches from our faces.

"Hello," Liza greets them. "We thought you were lost."

Their black eyes seem to sparkle with

cleverness. As if they can understand what we say.

With a shudder I think of the dead humming bird. The one in Father's study. It had horrid glass eyes. Like a lifeless doll's.

The front door slams again. Our heads whip round. The humming birds whisk away.

Father is already crossing the drawing room. Liza waits until he is inside the conservatory. Then dashes out behind him. She is going to hide in the kitchen. Leaving me to face Father alone.

Immediately, he begins searching among the flowers.

"Ah, Marianne," he says as if he has only just noticed me. "Where are my specimens?"

He casts his eye about to find them. His bony fingers push big, fat leaves aside.

I see a flash of gold. The humming birds are in their little straw house. I turn my eyes away quickly so Father won't follow my gaze.

"What do you want with them, Father?" I ask him, trying to keep my voice steady.

He looks surprised that I'm questioning him. But he is still in a good mood. So he answers me.

"I wish to study their feeding habits. Did I not say so?"

"You wish to observe them, Father? Sit here and watch them as I do?"

"No," Father smiles at my ignorance. "I wish to take them to my study. Then open them up, examine the contents of their stomachs. By such means I shall prove that I am right. For I expect to find samples of *Coleoptera*, that is, the beetle family, inside them."

He casts his sharp eyes about.

My heart is shrinking inside me, like the poor, shrivelled heart in his study.

I must find a way to stop him.

His brow grows dark with irritation.

"Where are they?" he says. "I am ready for

them now. I have been to get a fresh supply of cyanide for my killing jar."

"Please don't take them to your study, Father. Don't put them in your killing jar."

But he doesn't hear me. For he has just spotted them, in their little house, where I told them they were safe.

"Ahhh," he says, smiling in satisfaction. "There you are! I have found you out at last."

Chapter 11
Tiny Knights

"Father, you can't mean to do it. Please, I beg you, let them live. They are such little treasures. Don't put them in your killing jar."

Father stops and looks at me, astonished. He can't believe I would dare defy him.

There is a clattering sound behind me. It's Liza. She hasn't run away after all.

She's creeping back in, with a fresh tray of tea. But her hands are shaking so much that the tea things are going *clink, clink, clink.*

"Tea, Reverend Doctor Moxton?" she says.

"There is some cake, too."

But he says, "Not now, girl, not now," waving her away. "Go back to your kitchen."

He looks up into the banana tree.

"I need the short ladder," he mutters to himself. And he whisks about and strides into the garden.

"Oh, Miss," says Liza. "Please stop him."

Father strides back in. He has a short ladder. He is so fired up, so eager to get the birds that he doesn't even notice Liza has disobeyed his orders.

"Go back," I hiss to her. "Before he sees you."

But Liza shakes her head grimly. "I won't Miss. I won't leave you alone."

Father places the ladder against the banana tree.

I can't bear it. I hurl myself forwards and cling to his cloak.

"Father, Father, please let them live."

"Get away, rebellious child! How dare you oppose my wishes?"

He shakes me off. He is roaring now as he roars at his congregation in church. His gooseberry eyes are bulging with anger.

"Please, Master," says Liza.

"Silence, girl!" he roars at her. "I told you your place was in the kitchen! If you cannot learn to know your place then you shall lose it! Pack your bags instantly. Be gone from this house!"

"Father, please. Don't send her away. We are friends!"

That makes Father's rage even greater.

"Friends! What is all this nonsense? What has been happening while I have been away? We shall see about this, Marianne. As soon as I have these birds. . ."

In a cold fury he whips his cloak aside. Then steps on to the ladder.

I feel my heart will burst with pain. Eliza is weeping, "Oh Master, have pity!"

But Father has only to stretch out his hand and close the door of the straw cage. Then he will have them.

"Fly away!" I warn the humming birds desperately. "Fly away! He is your enemy!"

Father's eyes are gleaming. "Aha!" he cries in triumph. "I have you!"

He reaches out long, bony fingers to shut the cage and trap them inside.

But suddenly my humming birds come darting out.

They are like winged furies. Like tiny knights going into battle, their armour flashing crimson, green and gold.

One stabs at Father's head. The other flies straight for his eyes. With shrill chirps it darts at his face again and again.

My father is furious. He can't believe such tiny creatures would dare attack him. He waves them away, as if they were wasps.

But they are not afraid of him.

They dive in under his waving arms. He roars at them in a voice like thunder.

"Away, away, you demons!"

But they strike at him, drawing blood, as if they know him for their enemy.

"Father!" I cry.

My hands fly to my mouth. I can't move. I'm frozen to the spot with horror.

They dart in again, with fiery eyes. They jab him with needle-sharp beaks. My father howls at them, tries to shield his face. As he does so, he loses his hold on the ladder. The ladder sways. His feet are slipping.

"Master, take care...!" Eliza shrieks out a warning.

Too late.

My father tumbles down. It is not far to fall. But he strikes his head on the edge of the stone bench.

We rush forward. Father is motionless. His face is ghastly grey.

"Father! Father!"

My father groans once. Then he does not stir.

"I'll run next door and get help, Miss," says Liza, leaping up. "They'll know what to do."

"Run fast," I beg her. "Oh, please run fast!"

I can't believe what has happened. Father was a very important man. His will was so strong. It seemed to fill the whole world.

I can still hear his voice in my head: "Rebellious child!"

How can he be lying so helpless? It can't be possible. I must be dreaming.

Every second, I expect him to raise his head and open his eyes and say, "Marianne, what are you staring at? Attend to your duties."

But he doesn't raise his head. His eyes stay closed.

Liza comes racing back in. Her pale moon face is pink with running. Her voice is breathless.

"They're coming, Miss. They're bringing the doctor!"

Then Liza and I cling together. We have to, or we might fall down. We can't take our eyes off my father. We stare and stare, too shocked to speak.

Above our heads my humming birds whizz to and fro like shooting stars.

When some people come bursting in, we are still clinging together. The doctor is with them. He kneels by my father. He makes an examination. Then sighs and shakes his head. Some men lift my father up and carry him upstairs.

People are speaking to me, asking me things. But I can't answer. The doctor stoops down and looks into my face – his eyes are kind. He is asking me something, too. But I can't answer any of them. I am sure I must be dreaming. I will wake up soon.

Chapter 12
Our Most Secret Secret

I didn't wake up. What was happening was real.

When they carried him upstairs, Father was still breathing. But there was little hope. He had hit his head a dreadful blow.

Other doctors came. A famous doctor came all the way from London. But he could do no more than our village doctor.

My father never came to his senses. He died at midnight on the next day. His funeral was on Thursday morning at 11 o'clock. Many people came. Father was a very important man.

Shall I say my feelings? My *secret* feelings?

I don't know if I dare.

You see, they all think I'm grieving for Father. I've got black frills on my dress and bonnet.

Everyone in the village says, "Oh, what a tragedy. Poor little Miss!"

But I don't feel as sorry as a good child should. It seems shocking to say it. But I feel – a strange freedom.

My heart needn't tremble any more at his footsteps. Or the sound of his carriage wheels on the drive.

I can wear Mother's locket outside my clothes. I needn't hide it away. I'm wearing it now, for all the world to see.

After Father died I was sent to bed to rest. But I couldn't sleep. I felt so cold, then so hot and shivery.

I thought: God is punishing me for not caring

enough about Father. I am a bad child. I'm going to be very ill. I'll probably die.

I told Eliza: "I'm going to die."

She said, "Stuff and nonsense, Miss. You ain't dying. More likely it's just a chill. I know a recipe – lemons and honey in hot water. That'll cure it."

Liza knows cures for everything.

And she must have been right because I am still shaky. But today I feel a great deal better.

Liza is standing next to me among the parcels and boxes. She has on her best bonnet. We are all packed up, waiting in the driveway. Any moment now the cart is coming. We are going to live at Aunt Hettie's.

"Miss!" says Liza, poking me with her elbow.

"Ouch!"

"You are in a dreamy mood, Miss!"

"I'm thinking what it will be like at Aunt Hettie's," I tell her.

"It will be bliss, Miss Marianne. Just bliss."

Liza's little moon face is all lit up with smiles.

"I shan't have to get up in the cold and dark to light the fires. That's right, Miss, ain't it? I'm not a servant no more?"

She can't believe it. Though I've told her a thousand times. She can't believe she's going to Aunt Hettie's as my companion, not as a servant.

"That's right, Liza. You needn't wait on anyone. Only you mustn't call me Miss, neither. You are my friend. You must call me Marianne."

"Just think, Miss, I mean Marianne, my hands won't be red no more. They will be white like a fine lady's. And I shall be fat as butter at Aunt Hettie's. Not like a skinny scarecrow."

"And no one will stop us talking together at Aunt Hettie's. I expect you may have pink satin drawers if you want them."

"Satin drawers! I shan't know meself," says

Liza, hugging herself with delight. "I'll be like a princess. I won't have to do no cleaning. Aunt Hettie's will be like Heaven!"

And I'll go to school and be able to talk about my mother whenever I like. Aunt Hettie will tell me all about her. What she was like when she was a girl.

I should be as happy as Liza. I think I will be, in time, when Father's death isn't so much in my thoughts.

"I hope that cart is here soon," I tell Liza. "The humming birds don't like being shut up."

They are back in their nest in the hamper. But only for a short while, until we get to Aunt Hettie's.

Aunt Hettie has a big conservatory. It is big as a house. She said, "Your humming birds are welcome here, the little pets."

She doesn't know what part the humming birds had in Father's death. No one knows but me and Liza. It is our most secret secret. We shall never, never tell.

"My poor heart's fluttering something terrible," says Liza. "I'm that excited!"

I try to smile back at her. But, all of a sudden, I start to cry instead! I cry and cry as if my heart will break.

"There, there, there," says Liza, putting her arm round my shoulders. "Poor Marianne, you have had too many shocks. It's more than a body can bear. You are quite worn out! It will be all right once we are at Aunt Hettie's."

I know it will. But I still can't stop crying.

"Silly goose," I scold myself.

I dry my eyes and try to stop sniffling.

"Here is that cart!" cries Liza, hopping about. "I thought it would never come!"

The driver loads our baggage in the back of the cart.

He tries to take the humming-bird hamper from me.

"No," I tell him, holding it tight. "I'll keep this one with me, if you please."

"What's inside it, the crown jewels?" he asks me.

"Mind your own business," says Liza.

"Oh, highty-tighty, Miss!" says the driver.

Liza shoots up her eyebrows at me. And grins a big, mischievous grin. But still I can't seem to smile.

We sit in front with the driver, with the humming-bird hamper across our knees. The driver says, "Git on now," to the horses. Then we are off.

Soon, our old house is left far behind us.

"Do you think the humming birds will like it at Aunt Hettie's?" Liza asks me.

I think about them in Aunt Hettie's conservatory. They'll be safe there from scalpels and killing jars.

They'll light up the whole place with their sparkle.

A moment ago I couldn't smile at all. But now a little smile tickles my face. I can feel it.

"Oh, yes," I tell Liza. "I'm sure they will like it there. They will like it there as much as we do."